Carapace

by
David Mitchell Robinson

A SAMUEL FRENCH ACTING EDITION

SAMUEL
FRENCH

FOUNDED 1830

SAMUELFRENCH.COM

ISBN 978-0-573-70031-6   Printed in U.S.A.   #20267

MUSIC USE NOTE

IMPORTANT BILLING AND CREDIT REQUIREMENTS

CARAPACE received its world premiere at the Alliance Theatre in Atlanta, GA, on February 11, 2011, under the direction of Susan V. Booth, artistic director; with dramaturgy by Celise Kalke, scenic and costume design by Lex Liang, lighting design by John Ambrosone, sound design by Clay Benning, stage management by Rodney Williams, general management by Max Leventhal, company management by Laura Thurston, and production management by Rixon Hammond. The director was Judith Ivey. The cast was as follows:

JEFF	David de Vries
MARGO	Bethany Anne Lind
TED	Mark Kincaid
KYLE	Paul Hester
PETER	Joe Knezevich
BRIAN	Tony Larkin

CARAPACE was the winner of the 2010 Kendeda Graduate Playwriting Competition.

CHARACTERS

JEFF - a sports anchor – Mid-50s

MARGO - Jeff's daughter - 23

TED - Jeff's friend - Early 50s

KYLE - a pet store employee

PIZZA GUY - Mid-20s

PETER - Jeff's ex-brother-in-law - Late-30s

BRIAN - Margo's boyfriend, Mid-20s

WAITER - Mid-20s

NOTES ON MARGO'S SPEECH

Generally speaking, Margo's stutter affects the beginning of a given sentence but not the duration. If she can start the sentence, she's often in the clear, although we see her at different comfort/ability levels throughout the play.

Hyphenated repeat letters, [T-t-t-t-turtle], should be read as a single syllable repeated in quick succession (i.e. "Tuh-tuh-tuh-tuh-turtle").

Letters that are repeated without hyphenation [such as nnnnnno] should be read as an extended, monosyllabic consonant sound.

A parenthetical ellipsis [(...)] denotes a complete inability to speak, sometimes a slight croak, sometimes an extended inhalation (as though, she's preparing to speak for a loooong time).

(The set is a fragmented Oldsmobile Royale. Downstage center is the cabin: driver and passenger seats, a steering wheel and a backseat. Various chunks of the car are arranged throughout the stage. The stage has multiple headlights. Pieces of twisted metal and colored fiberglass should describe the three different performance spaces that surround the Oldsmobile cabin downstage center.)

(At stage right, there is a glass counter and display case, with a cash register, credit card scanner, etc. There is a door with a glass inset. There is another such door on the stage left side, which resembles a study. Also featured in this space is a large hanging map of the Twin Cities Metro Area.)

(Upstage center of the Oldsmobile cabin is a dining room: table, chairs and a hutch. Stretching from the stage right store to the upstage center Dining Room, there is a shelf full of aquariums and terrariums, each filled with its own assortment of fish, newts, crayfish, turtles, etc.)

*(As the play begins - and as it should be whenever **JEFF** is driving his car - the on-stage headlights should be illuminated. There is a travel mug with a tea tag hanging out of it in the console.)*

*(**JEFF** takes a deep breath and releases it.)*

JEFF. My daughter Margo's suffered from a terrible stutter since she first started kindergarten. Like: really terrible; like: incapacitatingly terrible. And she used to have this trick where she'd take a deep breath, close her eyes, let all the thoughts flash through and then count to seven to focus them before opening her eyes and saying whatever it was she'd intended to say. Right now, as I look out my passenger's side window at Margo's front door, I'm thinking maybe it might not hurt to try the same thing.

7

JEFF. *(cont.)* When I knock on that door tonight to give Margo the turtle I got her for her twenty-third birthday, I definitely don't expect to be received with open arms. But I need to do it. See, I used to pick Margo up from middle school every day, and we had this little ritual, where she'd walk up to the passenger's side of my Lexus and say, "Hey, Pops." And I'd ask, "What kind of shot was today?" And depending on whether her day had been good or bad, she'd either say "slam dunk" or "air ball." If we had an "air ball" on our hands, I'd call in late to work and we'd go for a drive so she could talk about her day. So, it was on one of those drives that she asked me, "Dad, am I always going to talk like this?"

And, like any father would, I said to her, "No, you won't, Margo. I promise: if there's anything in my power that I can do to help you, I will." So, if I'm going to make good on that promise, I'm going to have to focus *my* thoughts and pick out *just* the right thing to say.

*(**JEFF** closes his eyes. A twenty year-old **MARGO** enters and walks past **JEFF**, towards the counter.)*

MARGO. Yyyyyou're not d-d-driving. Get in the passenger's seat.

*(At the counter, **MARGO** gathers a number of pill bottles into a bag as **JEFF** continues to speak. **JEFF** moves from the driver's seat to the passenger's seat.)*

JEFF. *(to audience)* This is Margo at age twenty. It's three years ago. Now, listen carefully. In situations like this one, I find that someone like Margo will usually give somebody they love three outs – three chances to say the just right thing. So, just wait for it.

*(**MARGO** returns to the car and gets into the driver's seat. He doesn't make eye contact with **MARGO**.)*

MARGO. Your shoes…

*(**JEFF** takes his shoes. **MARGO** gets settled in the car, setting the bag in her lap so that she can buckle her seatbelt.)*

(JEFF *reaches for the bag of personal items, but* **MARGO**
doesn't let him have it and places it in the backseat.)

MARGO. No. Thhhhese can go in the back until I d-d-drop
you off. Your k-k-keys are in there, too.

(**MARGO** *starts the car.* Backstreets* *by Bruce
Springsteen comes over the stereo.*)

(**MARGO** *shuts the stereo off.*)

MARGO. Yyyyou know when I figured out you were d-drink-
ing again? It was t-t-two months ago, right before Andy
broke up with me. And you met us for lunch - not even
d-d-dinner - *lunch.* And you k-k-kept asking him how
his chemistry classes were going, making sssssstupid
jokes about half-lives. Aaaaand I told you a hundred
times: "It's *B-b-b-biology,* Dad. Not Chemistry." See,
other than that it's hard to tell if you're drinking. B-b-
b-but, you forget. You mistake these little things you
never would otherwise, like the name of where I work
or my birthday.

Yyyyyou have the opportunity t-t-to apologize, you
know. Or t-t-tell me anything I'm nnnnot "understanding."

(**MARGO** *looks to him for a reply.* **JEFF** *says nothing.*)

MARGO. No? Yyyyou know, I had p-p-plans tonight for
once. With a girl from school. And I was sssso excited.
Until I heard from Mmmom that you're in d-d-detox
again – that you almost died. And I said to her, "Llllllet
me c-c-cancel my plans and I'll p-p-pick him up." How
was I supposed to mmmmake sssmall talk at d-d-dinner
when the only thing on my mind was huge? Hhhhow
was I supposed to fit it in? Sssssssee, I c-c-can't count
on anything – can't *have* anything – because of you.
Aaaaand if I wwwwwwwwww...

One... Two... Three...

If I ever want to have anything again, I c-c-c-can't see
you anymore. I can't t-t-talk to you. I c-c-can't have any
c-c-cards. Or birthday gifts (not that you'd remember).

---

* See Music Use Note on page 3.

MARGO. *(cont.)* Otherwise, I'll just end up sssssstupidly getting my hopes up and letting my guard d-d-down and I can't afford to do that again. And I d-d-don't want you paying my rent anymore. I nnnneed a new home – a p-p-place I c-can feel comfortable in b-because I know it's *mine* – that I'm safe there.

Unless – and, again, yyyou have the opportunity – you can t-t-tell me why I shouldn't do this. Why I should b-b-believe that you're really, t-t-truly going to get sober – that you're really going to try…

(**MARGO** *looks to him for a reply.* **JEFF** *says nothing.*)

(**MARGO** *pulls over to the curb and puts the car in park.*)

MARGO. Hhhhhhere's your house. IIIIII assume this is where you want to get d-dropped off.

(**MARGO** *looks at him once more.*)

MARGO. Thhhhhis might b-b-be the last time you see me, Dad. Iiiiiis there anything you want to say to me?

(**JEFF** *takes a deep inhale and looks at her. The exhaustion of detox can be heard in his voice.*)

JEFF. I… The house is fine…

(*He looks back down at the shoes in his lap.*)

MARGO. "The house is ffffine…." *(beat)* Get out, please.

(**JEFF** *gets out of the car.*)

JEFF. That's right. "The house is fine…"

That was the last time we spoke. Three years later and I still haven't seen my own daughter.

After that, I got a benchmark case of the "rock bottoms." Ended up in the hospital again. It was a few months after that that I took an emergency medical leave from the station - I'm a sports anchor at KSTP, Channel Nine - and got down with a little extended recovery at Hazelden, which is like the porterhouse of the recovery world. Got out. Did the outpatient care my ex-wife Melissa always wanted me to do. And, then I got well.

During my Fourth Step "searching moral inventory" phase, I unearthed a letter from Margo... One from shortly before she cut me off.

(*JEFF pulls out a letter. MARGO reads its contents to him.*)

MARGO. The problem with men, in my book, is that they're either so stoic that they withhold and don't open up about *anything*, or they take note that you're a woman and they assume that you want to listen to them yammer endlessly. You, Dad, somehow manage to do both.

Because when you drink–

JEFF. Okay, that's probably enough.

(**MARGO** *gets up and exits.* **JEFF** *watches her walk off and then whispers to the audience so that this memory of* **MARGO** *won't hear.*)

JEFF. *(whispered)* I've never told her this. But she's right. I *am* a withholder. *(aloud)* As for how I manage to embody *both* poles on the masculine-communicatory-failure-spectrum, we'll get to that.

But as far as my reticence goes... When you're in recovery, they - and by "they" I mean everybody - really jam that butter knife in and try to pry you open and get your story to spill out.

(*JEFF swivels his seat out to face the passenger side.*)

JEFF. Don't ask me why; it's just not my style. I never really understood the value of it. I mean, intellectually or abstractly, yeah. But, I never really, innately, emotionally, felt like I understood that.

(**TED** *enters, swivels the driver's seat to face the passenger's side, pulls a table between them and takes a seat.* **JEFF** *stares at a wall-mounted TV.* **TED** *has a Rolling Rock in front of him,* **JEFF** *a soda.*)

JEFF. That is, until earlier today.

TED. You're pretty smitten with that TV.

JEFF. This is Ted. He's a former Minneapolis AA; and he's actually my ex-wife Melissa's sister Crystal's ex-husband – so: technically my twice-exed-ex-brother-in-law, but why bother with all the terminology, right? We were never even that close when we were legally-speaking still in the same family, but today he calls me up and tells me he needs to meet me on my four-thirty break and talk to me about something.

TED. Why's your station showing all that footage of the bridge? Story's four months old.

JEFF. This is the kind of thing Channel Nine does at the end of the year. You take something awful, like the 35-W bridge collapse and give it a… hopeful human-interest gloss.

TED. Seems to work well enough on you. It's got you all gauzy.

JEFF. Well, Ted, I live in Edina and Margo lives across the river there on the East Bank. The metaphor's just kind of irresistible.

Look at those pathetic little sticks reaching out from either side of the river.

TED. They're called abutments. Speaking of abutments, why don't you sit yours down?

(**JEFF** *sits down in the passenger's seat, across from* **TED**.)

TED. So. Why you being like this?

JEFF. Sorry. It's Margo's birthday. I always get a little down on-

TED. I'm not talking about being down. I'm talking about being the kind of guy who stands by on his daughter's birthday and lets "Peter" give the dad gifts.

JEFF. What's a "dad gift?"

TED. Dad gift. The gift from the older male figure in her life. You're gonna let Melissa's prick little brother horn in on your kid just 'cause he's not procreating?

JEFF. *(to audience)* Peter's my *other* ex-brother-in-law. Mel's brother. How I ever got to have so many ex-brothers-in-law is beyond me.

TED. Little faggot always walking around in his robe like he's Joan Crawford.

JEFF. What are you talking about? It's not like that. He's... It's a moot point. I can't give Margo anything. She won't see me.

TED. I heard you pay her rent. That true?

JEFF. Through Melissa, yeah. She doesn't know that, though.

TED. But you can't go over there.

JEFF. No.

TED. Pff. That is retarded. And I can say that. I got a kid's half-retarded.

JEFF. He's dyslexic, Ted.
Look, you said you had something you needed to talk about? I should really get back to work.

TED. Hey! Shut up. Come on: stay on the same road as me. Now, why can't you go over there?

JEFF. Ted, I don't want to talk about Margo, okay?

TED. You do this sad-sack	**JEFF**. You said you had some-
routine every year on	thing you wanted to
her birthday and go on	meet up about. Let's
about what a terrible	hear it. I'm not gonna sit
father you've been and	here and-
rah-bah-bah.	

TED. I saw her.

JEFF. What? Margo? You did?

TED. That's what I called you about. Last weekend at Crystal's wedding.

JEFF. Well? How is she? How's her speaking? Is she doing okay?

TED. Jeff, I got some bad news... She's gone silent again.

JEFF. What?

(*A* **WAITER** *comes along and takes their lunch plates.*)

WAITER. How we all doing, here?

TED. Yeah, everything was great. Can I get another Rolling Rock?

WAITER. Another Ro-Ro? No sweat. *(to* **JEFF***)* More Diet?

JEFF. No. Actually, I'll take one of those, too.

TED. Fuck are you doing? *(to* **WAITER***)* He doesn't drink.

JEFF. Ted, it's one beer. I'm an adult. *(to* **WAITER***)* It's fine.

WAITER. Done and done.

(**WAITER** *exits*)

JEFF. Now, wait: what do you mean she's gone silent? She's not talking? Are you sure?

TED. Here I am trying to talk to her – just ask her how life's going – and I couldn't get a mouse squeak out of her. She didn't talk to anyone the whole reception; I asked people. Her own *family*. Jeff, it's just like the last time.

JEFF. Not talking at all? Why? What happened?

TED. I don't know. Tried to ask Mel about it, but you know her – she never thinks anything's a problem. Which is why this is on you. You've gotta go over there. Today. For her birthday. I mean, unless you're interested in letting her fucking boyfriend help her through this.

JEFF. Boyfriend? She has a boyfriend?

TED. Yeah. You didn't know?

JEFF. Well, Ted, I find that when girls cut off all contact with a parent, they don't tend to offer a lot of updates on their romantic lives. They definitely don't want you showing up unannounced.

TED. Well, I'm sorry if your teenage daughter who-

JEFF. She's twenty-three.

TED. Who you *pay rent for* and who's going through a crisis needs you to keep your distance. But what she needs is a little more important than what she needs. You know what I mean?

JEFF. I mean, if she's got a boyfriend, I guess she's got someone she can talk to, right?

TED. This kid's not the solution. If anything, he's a part of the fucking problem.

JEFF. Why do you say that?

TED. They met at an Al-Anon meeting.

JEFF. What's that supposed to mean? Al-Anon's important. Families of drunks like you and me need something to keep them sane-

TED. Al-Anon has the same rules as AA. You're not supposed to date the people you meet in that shit. They have that rule for a reason.

JEFF. You'd know.

TED. Well, first off: shut the fuck up; this isn't about me. But second: put yourself in that meeting, Jeff. You're looking across the church basement at some girl with a stutter who's crying her little eyes out about her drunk dad. What kind of parasite's thinking to himself, "Damn, I gotta get a number"?

JEFF. Yeah, but-

TED. Plus he dragged her out of the reception early. And you know you can't trust a guy gets between family.

JEFF. Seriously?

TED. So, I'm sure he'd be happy having everyone think there is no problem. Now, listen – and I say this with double-exed brotherly love – you're the one who fucked her up and you're the one who has to fix this thing.

JEFF. Thanks, Ted. Really, thanks.

TED. Come on, man. I'm not saying anything controversial here. And I only feel like I can say that because I tend to fuck things up about eleven times what you do. Plus – and we both know this is true – you never fuck anything up more than once or twice. Why the fuck you think they call you "The Two-Take Titan" at the studio?

JEFF. Ted, I don't know. We haven't spoken in-

TED. Ninth Step is making *direct* amends.

JEFF. "Except when to do so would injure them or others."

TED. "Injure them?" How are you gonna injure anybody? You've got to get over the idea of doing something well and realize that dads are always the ones pulling a Tarkenton and-

JEFF. Pulling a Tarkenton is when you fuck up *three* times.

TED. No, it's not.

JEFF. Ted, that's my phrase. I made it up. I think I know what it means.

TED. Whatever. Dads are always the ones wrecking shit. That's what makes a dad gift a real dad gift: it's always kind of an apology.

JEFF. Tell me about it.

(*The* **WAITER** *returns with two Rolling Rocks and sets them on the table.*)

WAITER. Heeeeere y'go.

(*The* **WAITER** *exits.* **TED** *takes his first sip.* **JEFF** *just looks at his bottle.*)

(*Finally,* **JEFF** *lifts his beer.*)

TED. Hey. Just one, right? You got shit to do today.

JEFF. Yeah. Just one.

(**JEFF** *takes his first sip.*)

TED. Well, look... Let me tell you something.

(**JEFF** *stands up and addresses the audience again.*)

JEFF. And that's when it happens. For the first time in the twenty years we've known each other, Ted tells me his story. About how sorely he fucked things up with his ex-wife Crystal and their two kids. How painful it was to know that Crystal was one of the only people looking out for him and to feel like the outsider at her wedding. He tells me in painstaking detail. And I'm floored. Here's a guy I've never given any reason to open up to me... and he's spilling his guts.

And I get all blubbery, because when this ex-familial non-friend is telling me his story, I'm hearing *mine*. And suddenly, for the first time, I'm telling *my* story. And, all of a sudden - I don't know for sure about Ted, but I know for sure about me - it feels okay. Just *telling* these things makes it feel like they're not the hugest things in the world. If just telling people things can *do this*, I start to think maybe what Ted's saying isn't such a bad idea.

TED. So, what's your plan?

JEFF. *(to TED)* You know, I was always going to save them for her; but I do have all these letters I've written to her over the past three years. But, they're all really long and disorganized. I could maybe put some of it in an e-mail.

TED. No. E-mail's for someone who wants to hide. I'm telling you. Actions speak louder than words.

JEFF. Actions speak louder than words. I think I've got it. I think I know what I'm gonna do.

(TED gets out of the driver's seat and the two of them swivel the seats back into driving position.)

TED. I'm glad. Hey, it's been too long, man. We should do this again sometime.

JEFF. Yeah, we should. Wish me luck today.

(TED gives JEFF a big hug.)

TED. Yeah. Good luck. Just don't do anything I wouldn't do.

JEFF. I might need to do a little better than that.

TED. This fucking guy…

(TED exits)

JEFF. *(to audience)* My plan was really simple. Check it out…

(JEFF crosses to the Twin Cities map, on which he traces his voyage and he speaks.)

JEFF. I'd leave my house in Edina at seven twenty so that I could get everything in time to show up at Margo's before her birthday officially ended. So on my way up there, I'd just stop here in St. Louis Park to pick up a tortoise, Margo's very favorite reptile. Then, I'd stop here in Golden Valley to sneak into my ex-wife's house to grab my old, busted-up terrarium. (I've got the glue and glass I need to fix it up in the trunk.) Also at Melissa's house is that god-awful-ugly-red-leather address book–

(JEFF *gestures to the hutch in the dining room. Sure enough, there's a bright red address book.*)

JEFF. –that you can see right over there on Melissa's hutch. That's where I'd get Margo's address (which I'm not allowed to have) since I knew Mel'd be out of town and wouldn't know that I'd come over.

Also, in the interest of full-disclosure, although I didn't know it when I left Edina, I'd pull off at a liquor store to buy and consume a small helping of Maker's Mark right there, right there and right there.

(*Lights up on the stage right door and counter set-up. Enter* KYLE. *He's in his mid-twenties and is an employee at George's Pets. As* JEFF *is narrating,* KYLE *walks to the glass door upstage right and flips the door's sign to closed.*)

(JEFF *empties an airplane-sized bottle of Maker's Mark into his travel mug and downs it.*)

JEFF. Phew. The first of those three "right theres" delayed my arrival at George's Pets, which - God bless George, whoever he is - was the only pet store on my way that was open 'til eight. I just wanted that one tiny, little airplane bottle to settle me down a bit. Because I don't want to cause any trouble tonight. I just want to open up to Margo. All I want to do is put this terrarium together with her and just *relate* to her. Tell her that I know what it's like to be locked up inside of yourself. To not be able to talk.

(JEFF *notices the turning of the sign just as* KYLE *is throwing the deadbolt to lock the door.* JEFF *lifts himself out of the seat and hurries to the door.*)

JEFF. Shit. Hey, hey, hey!

(KYLE *tries to ignore the sound and starts sweeping his space.* JEFF *makes it to the door and peers through.*)

JEFF. Hey! Did you guys just close?

> (*When* KYLE *doesn't respond,* JEFF *raps on the door.*)

> C'mon. I know you can hear me.

> (KYLE *crosses and addresses* JEFF *through the glass.*)

KYLE. Closed, buddy. Sorry.

JEFF. No, listen. I know exactly what I need. I won't be five minutes.

KYLE. No can do, man. Come on...

JEFF. It's my daughter's birthday, alright? You got any kids?

KYLE. We're open again at eleven tomorrow.

JEFF. It's...

> (JEFF *checks his watch.*)

JEFF. Look, it's only her birthday for another four hours. I can't come back tomorrow.

KYLE. Listen, man, I've got a place I need to get to. You gonna make it worth my while?

JEFF. Worth your... Are you serious?

> (KYLE *checks his watch.*)

KYLE. Three-hours, fifty-five minutes, actually.

JEFF. Shit. Fine. Alright...

> (JEFF *pulls out his wallet.*)

JEFF. Make it worth your while...

> (JEFF *plasters a twenty dollar bill against the glass.* KYLE *opens the door and takes the twenty.* JEFF *walks in.*)

KYLE. You said five minutes. Are you gonna be trouble?

JEFF. Are you going to extort me any more?

KYLE. "Extort." You're funny, you know that?

JEFF. Seriously, thank you so much. Hey, what's your name, guy?

KYLE. Kyle.

JEFF. Kyle. Thank you. I'm Jeff.

KYLE. Cool. Well, clock's ticking, Jeff. What're you looking for?

JEFF. I'm putting together a terrarium. I need a tortoise. If I remember, I need a heat lamp and a timer for one of those, right?

KYLE. Yeah. Alright, you take a look at the reptiles and I'll grab you the gear you need. Right over there.

(*JEFF goes and looks at the bay of aquariums.* **KYLE** *goes behind the display case and starts placing a few items on the counter.*)

JEFF. Jeez. These guys are great.

KYLE. You know…you look familiar. Are you on TV or something?

JEFF. Uh…can't say as I am.

KYLE. You could've fooled me with that hair, you know? Got that crispy, spiky thing going on. You know what kind of enclosure you wanna buy?

JEFF. No, I already have a terrarium. It's about the size of this one here. Exactly like this.

(*JEFF points to one of the display aquariums.*)

KYLE. It's a fish tank? I hope you're looking to get a juvenile, 'cause that's not really big enough for a mature—

JEFF. Yeah. A baby tortoise is what I'm looking for.

KYLE. It's just best if it's wide and shallow. And that fish tank's not gonna last long before your tortoise gets—

JEFF. I'm sure your enclosures are nice; I just figure I've already got—

KYLE. It's not about selling you an enclosure. I just wanna make sure you're gonna make a good home for it. You will, right? Don't bullshit me.

JEFF. Of course.

KYLE. And, when it gets bigger, you'll have to build it something bigger. I gotta make sure we're crystal on this.

JEFF. Yeah. We're crystal.

KYLE. Alright. I'm throwing some Cypress Mulch in here, too. I'm out of warm mist humidifiers right now. But you should really get one of those as soon as possible.

(A particular tortoise catches **JEFF**'s *eye.)*

JEFF. Got it. Hey, this is a handsome looking fellow.

KYLE. Lady.

JEFF. Yeah? Even better. How much?

KYLE. Fine specimen, isn't she? That's a Cherry Head Red-Footed Tortoise. That tortoise costs two hundred, ninety-nine dollars. Being as it's your daughter's birthday, I could let her go for two, seventy-five.

JEFF. Jesus Christ! Are you serious?

KYLE. Well, don't gimme that look. They're special animals. What'd you expect?

JEFF. What about the Honey Colored, here?

KYLE. Two, twenty-five.

JEFF. Whoa.

KYLE. What? That out of your price range?

JEFF. No, um. Prices have just changed since 1999.

KYLE. Daughter's birthday, man. *(laughs)* Know what I mean? When else do dads pull out all the stops?

JEFF. Right. Anyway, if I'm going above two hundred, I might as well buy this one here. She's beautiful.

KYLE. The Cherry? Good choice. Yeah, that's fine. So, what's your daughter's name?

JEFF. Margo.

KYLE. Margo. That's nice... Wait...
Holy shit!

JEFF. What?

KYLE. I *do* know you.

JEFF. I'm not so sure, buddy.

KYLE. No. I *do*.

JEFF. Alright, you got me. But, before you go asking who the Twins are going to trade Santana to, I gotta tell you—

KYLE. What are you talking about?

JEFF. Channel 9. That's where you know me. *(beat)* I'm the sports anchor.

KYLE. I don't watch Channel 9.

JEFF. Well, then I think you might be mist—

KYLE. Were you at Hazelden?

(*Beat.* JEFF *stops in his tracks.*)

JEFF. No. No.

KYLE. Don't fuckin' bullshit me, man. That was you. I know that was you. You were the one who never said shit in meeting.

JEFF. I...I don't know what you're talking about.

KYLE. No, no. Here: this was you in meeting...

(KYLE *does his impersonation of a stoic-faced* JEFF, *folding his arms and looking snide.*)

KYLE. All stoic and shit. Arms folded.

JEFF. Kyle. You're thinking of somebody else.

KYLE. Noooo. Me and that kid Rickie got you to play Yahtzee that one day. And when you loosened up a little we fuckin' bugged you to pull your pictures out of your wallet. And you told me to shut up 'cause I was like, "Damn, Jeff, you're daughter's fucking *fine*."

JEFF. Oh...gosh. Yeah. I suppose I do remember that.

KYLE. Sure, you do. Fuck, man. This is crazy.

JEFF. Yeah.

KYLE. Listen, sorry to be a dick about the close time. I've actually got an NA meeting at Grace Trinity I try to get to. What's with the subterfuge? Trying to convince me we didn't meet.

JEFF. Yeah, sorry. I didn't recognize you and since I'm on TV, I try to be discrete about my time in the pen. You know...

KYLE. Right. Sorry. I'm just kind of like blasé, blasé, what the fuck ever.
So, it's Margo's b-day. Wow. She looking for a date? Heyyyyyy. Just fucking with you.

JEFF. Right. You know, I got a letter from Rickie at one point. Seemed like he was doing well.

KYLE. Yeah, not so much.

JEFF. What do you mean?

KYLE. Kid came in here about six months ago. Talking to me, like, "Listen: I'm about to take a road trip and my cat gets real sick and, shit. Anyway, you work with animals, so I was wondering if you knew where I could get some Ketamine."

JEFF. Ketamine?

KYLE. Well, if you're a cat it's a tranquilizer. If you're a person, it's a Schedule III dissociative.

JEFF. Oh, jeez. So, what'd you do?

KYLE. Told him to get the fuck out of my store. Sucks. I've had a couple of Hazelden and NA people come in here looking for me hoping I could hook 'em up.

But, hey, check it out. Two and a half years next month.

JEFF. You know. That's a great accomplishment, man. That's gotta feel great.

(**JEFF** *extends his hand.* **KYLE** *shakes it.*)

KYLE. Yeah, well. Trick is, you gotta tell yourself two and a half years don't mean shit.

JEFF. How do you mean?

KYLE. Like, when you're looking too much at the past – doesn't matter if it's good stuff or bad stuff – you can't see when you're walking into a shit storm. So I always try to just be like, "Okay. This is what I'm doing right now. This is what I'm doing right now. This is what I'm doing right now." Otherwise I end up making the same dumb fucking mistakes over and over again.

JEFF. It's a "one day at a time" thing.

KYLE. But there's this crazy-ass thing that happens. When you do end up making the same dumb fucking mistakes and you're, like, "Shit, I keep *doing* this." Then bringing the past into the present is useful. Know what I mean?

JEFF. Kind of.

KYLE. Anyway. Recovery brain-twisters. Blah, blah, blah. How's life been for you?

JEFF. Good. Good, uh…

(JEFF *checks his watch.*)

JEFF. God, Kyle, you know, I hate to do this. But I should—

KYLE. Oh, shit. Yeah. Say no more.

(KYLE *gets behind the register.*)

JEFF. Yeah. So, what? Two, seventy-five for this one?

KYLE. Yeah.

JEFF. Sounds good.

KYLE. Huh… *(beat)* Hey, Jeff…

JEFF. Yeah?

KYLE. IIIIIIIII thought your daughter broke it off with you not long before you checked in to the Haze.

JEFF. Oh…right. Yeah, that was a rough spot there. No, we patched it up.

She was really supportive when I got out.

KYLE. Cool… so, where's she live?

JEFF. East Bank. Marcy-Holmes neighborhood.

KYLE. What street?

JEFF. Um…Cedar Avenue.

KYLE. Cedar Ave.? I wish you wouldn't have said that.

JEFF. Why?

(Beat. KYLE *exhales.*)

KYLE. Man, I've run enough mollies and speed around the U of M campus to know that Cedar… It doesn't run through Marcy-Holmes.

(JEFF *opens his wallet and pulls out his credit card.*)

JEFF. Here you go. How much for all the gear? Lamp and stuff?

KYLE. Got that lamp and timer… Fifty-three. Round it to fifty.

JEFF. And two, seventy-five for the beauty?

KYLE. Yeah. Uh… Look, man… I fucked up and forgot. That tortoise isn't for sale.

JEFF. Why?

KYLE. George has it on hold for someone, I think.

JEFF. Pet store layaway? Are you serious?

Shit. I guess I can take the Honey Colored. She's pretty, too.

KYLE. You know, when I think about it, we've actually got some really nice stuff over here you didn't really look at.

JEFF. Yeah?

KYLE. Sure. Check this out. Red-Ear Sliders, Yellow Bellies, Mississippi Maps. These are great for an aquarium anyway. You just dump rocks and-

JEFF. Wait. No, no, no. These are turtles. I wanted…

Kyle, what's the matter? Is there a problem here?

KYLE. No. It's just these turtles are-

JEFF. No, not a turtle. It has to be a tortoise.

KYLE. Come on, man…

(beat)

JEFF. This is bullshit.

KYLE. You said you weren't gonna be trouble.

JEFF. When I thought you were going to treat me like you would any other customer.

KYLE. It's below zero out there and you don't even know where you're going. Who knows how long she'll be in your car—

JEFF. I just don't have the address yet. I'm getting it from her mother right after I leave here.

KYLE. Right.

JEFF. I can get it any time I want.

KYLE. These aren't native animals. We shouldn't even be selling them in Minnesota. You want to come back with your daughter tomorrow so I can know for sure one of 'em'll have a good home, that's a different story.

JEFF. If it's not going to Margo's, I'm bringing it back to my place. So, what are you saying?

KYLE. Like I said, if you want to do something else, those Mississippi Maps are nice.

She lives near the river, right? It's perfect?

(Beat. JEFF *sighs.)*

JEFF. Alright. I'll take that one, there.

(KYLE *tries to lighten the mood a bit while he fishes the turtle out of the aquarium and place it in a little, opaque, plastic carton, which he then puts in a small paper bag.)*

KYLE. Hey, that's a nice choice, there, isn't it?

These run thirty. But, let's call it ten. I'll give you a little extortion refund since we're tight. What kind of pebbles you want? Pink rocks? Blue?

JEFF. I'll do blue.

(KYLE *punches the prices into the register.)*

KYLE. Good deal. I'm gonna need... Sixty bucks.

(KYLE *takes and swipes* JEFF*'s card. They wait.)*

KYLE. Machine takes a minute.

JEFF. So, let me ask you a question, Kyle.

(KYLE *puts the gear in a plastic bag.)*

KYLE. What's that?

JEFF. If you didn't recognize me, what would I be walking out of here with?

KYLE. It's my fault. Like I said: guys I know've come in here for one reason or another, saying they were on top of it all and wanting... I'm just not doing it again.

(The printer spits out a receipt.)

If you could sign that.

(JEFF *takes the pen but doesn't sign it.)*

JEFF. A baby tortoise was what I wanted to say to my daughter tonight. Trust me, on this because I speak from experience: taking away someone's ability to say something... That's the worst thing. You know that? The worst thing you can do.

(**KYLE** *has broken off debate and speaks to* **JEFF** *coolly.*)

KYLE. So, don't mess around on your way to wherever you're getting, okay? You've got to get this guy into an aquarium as soon as possible. Pile some rocks on one side and let the water climb up the glass to about this height.

JEFF. *(to audience)* My head was buzzing with all the things I wanted to explain to Kyle. That he didn't understand my situation. That whatever happened with those other Hazelden and NA people, it wasn't like that with me. And I turned to him and I said: *(to* **KYLE***)* Right... See you around, Kyle. Thanks for everything.

(*With aggravation,* **JEFF** *signs the receipt.*)

KYLE. Yeah. Good luck, pal.

(**JEFF** *leaves the pet store and* **KYLE** *locks the door behind him.* **KYLE** *exits as* **JEFF** *walks to his car, places the gear and the turtle bag in the back and walks around to the driver's side.*)

JEFF. Damn it.
And I do speak from experience. And as cute as that little Mississippi Map Turtle is, I find that I'm fairly bent out of shape over this. This is when I stop for the second of the three "right theres."

(**JEFF** *takes a seat in the cabin. He produces another airplane-sized bottle of Maker's Mark, pours it in his travel mug and savors it.*)

(*He then takes the wheel again and the headlights glow.*)

JEFF. Now before I explain why I decided to do that, I want to show you how I think Margo's stuttering works. So, we're going to do a little demonstration.
I'm sitting in my car looking at the closest intersection to Margo's house: Fourth Street and Fourth Avenue.

JEFF. *(cont.)* Okay, riiiiiiight *now* the stop light for Fourth
  Street just turned from red to green and the silver
  Volkswagen that had been stopped and revving its
  engine has just started rolling. So its front wheels are
  entering the first inch of intersection at...

  (JEFF checks his watch.)

  Ten fifteen, with the second hand at twenty-seven.

  *(JEFF gets up and crosses to the Twin Cities Map and
  uses a marker to draw an "X" on the southeast part of
  the intersection.)*

  (Next to the "X" he writes "10:15:27.")

JEFF. So you won't forget.
  Alright, now, of course I realize that the causes of
  stuttering are varied. But Margo's - the type of stuttering I'm talking about - comes when a person's got so
  many things racing around their internal race track
  that none of them can quite slow down fast enough to
  make the off ramp and get said.

  (MARGO enters.)

JEFF. Now, say your daughter's trying to say something to
  you. What's a good one?

MARGO. Don't tell me I'd be happier if I moved back in
  with you and Mom.

JEFF. But it comes out more like:

MARGO. D-d-d-d-d-d-d-d-d-on't tell me—

JEFF. Now when that first "duh" starts, everything's fine.
  But, all of a sudden, instead of the "duh" starting
  to bound gracefully into an "on't," something goes
  wrong.

  (MARGO sits down in the passenger's seat.)

JEFF. She starts thinking so much shit about you and what
  a terrible place you've made out of the house she grew
  up in and how it pisses her off so much that you'd dare

to tell her what a wonderful house it *could* be if she'd come back while you sit there sipping that cup that you let a tea tag dangle out of so she "won't know" it's just Maker's Mark. But as those thoughts – those thoroughly adult indictments – start spilling off the tongue, she can't help but envision how meager and decidedly *un*-adult they'll sound when *she* says them, so maybe she *shouldn't* say them or maybe she should say them a different way and on and on and on... See? When you've got all of that going on between the "duh" and the potential "on't," how do you get it all out at once? You don't. You just get "duh"s two through nine.

"Really?" you're thinking. She's thinking all that during that first "duh?" Well, remember when I started telling you everything I'm thinking right now?

(**JEFF** *checks his watch again and uses the marker to draw an "X" and write "10:15:30" on the other side of the intersection.*)

JEFF. Ten fifteen with the second hand at thirty. Three seconds.

And the rear wheels of that silver Volkswagen have *just* exited the other side of the intersection.

(**JEFF** *gets up out of the driver's seat and pulls it over to the desk.*)

Three seconds is the definition of small talk. But there's no such thing as small talk in here. If these thoughts were smaller, simpler, less tangled up, maybe I could've said more than "the house is fine." But, when I have a drink - even when it's as small as that second tiny bottle of Maker's Mark - I feel like I can take those three seconds with both hands and just stretch them out a little bit. It lets me fit more in. And if I'm gonna talk to Margo, really give her those tangled up thoughts, I need to fit more in.

(**JEFF** *seats himself at the desk.*)

JEFF. So, I think I mentioned the busted up terrarium in the trunk. To understand how it is that I'm going to talk to Margo, I need to tell you how I broke it in the first place. So, this was back during Margo's freshman year of high school. Melissa was out of town on business so it was just Margo and me around the house. So I was having a nice mid-evening "cup of tea." And, well…

(*He sniffs the teacup on the desk. He then pulls a tin of Altoids out of the desk drawer…*)

Smells like an Altoid night.

(*…and pops two in his mouth.* **MARGO** *walks up to his desk.*)

MARGO. Hey, P-p-p-pops. Wwwwhat are you doing?

(**JEFF** *swivels quickly in his chair and hides the mug behind him.*)

JEFF. Uhh…Nada mucho, senorita.

MARGO. You don't usually hang out in the study.

JEFF. Just paying some bills before the news comes on. What's up?

(**MARGO** *holds out a slip of paper.*)

MARGO. I nnneed you to sign this. Mmmmmom was going to, b-b-but I forgot to ask her b-before she left.

JEFF. What is it?

MARGO. Exception slip.

JEFF. "Exception slip?" What's it say?

MARGO. Sssssays I'm exceptional.

JEFF. Well, nobody needs my say-so on that. Lemme see it.

(**JEFF** *takes the piece of paper and reads it.*)

JEFF. This says you need to be excused from the presentation in Mr. Kapsner's class.

(**MARGO** *shrugs.*)

JEFF. Why?

MARGO. I can't.

JEFF. Why not? What's the presentation?

MARGO. T-t-t-t-talking about fffffeatures of different reptiles.

JEFF. What? You're always talking about how you want a terrarium like your cousin's. This is perfect.

MARGO. Wwwwwhat'd be p-p-p-perfect is if you let me have
one. Wwwwwe're, like, the only home I knnnnow without fish or reptiles or anything.

JEFF. You've come a long way, Margo.

MARGO. Hhhere with you and Mom, nnnnnnnn-n-not at
school. Only when I'm at *home*.

JEFF. Why?

MARGO. B-b-b-because I'm safe here.

JEFF. What?

MARGO. IIIIIII can hide. I c-c-can go to my room. And I
don't need to worry about those assholes who always—

JEFF. A., I don't want to hear you say that word, Margo.
And, B., you can't hide your whole life.

(**JEFF** *gestures to the house they're standing in.*)

JEFF. The world's not as little as our house. You're gonna
outgrow this whether you like it or not. You can't just
say what you have to say in here. If you want to say it
out there, you've got to start—

MARGO. Wwwwwwhy bother?

JEFF. How much do you love turtles and you don't want to
tell your class about them?

MARGO. T-t-tortoises.

JEFF. How big is the class?

(*She doesn't reply.*)

JEFF. Twenty people? Thirty? Thirty-fi-

MARGO. Twelve.

JEFF. Only twelve? Margo, that's perfect. You know that's
perfect. What'd we say about that? It's like your speech
therapist said. You have to find things that are in your
stretch zone but not in your panic zone.

MARGO. It's "stress zone," Dad. Not "stretch."

JEFF. Fine. What's the biggest number - speaking in class - what's the biggest number in your stress zone before it's your panic zone?

MARGO. Ten.

JEFF. Mmm, ten was your stress zone at the beginning of the school year, wasn't it?

MARGO. Fine. Eleven.

JEFF. Well, what's one more? *(beat)* Honey. Listen. I got something today.

(**JEFF** *reaches into his shoulder bag and pulls out an envelope.*)

JEFF. Can you guess what these are?

MARGO. No.

JEFF. I'll give you a hint. I got them for free from Tanya, the lady who does all the promotions.

MARGO. Wait...

JEFF. And they're for something happening at the Target Center.

MARGO. Bruce Springsteen tickets?!

JEFF. *(to audience)* See, this is why I love this kid. She's fourteen years old, it's 1999, and nobody in her school can shut up about Christina, Britney, and the fucking Goo Goo Dolls.

But Margo - she nearly blows a fuse over Boss tickets.

(to **MARGO***)* Yes, Margo. They are Bruce Springsteen tickets. Reunion tour. November 28th.

MARGO. Fffffor free? That's so... *(realizing the "deal")* Oh, no...

JEFF. Mm hm.

MARGO. D-d-dad! C-c-can't we just go and something else can be the prize or whatever?

JEFF. I will take you...but only if you agree to do the turtle presentation.

(**MARGO** *groans.*)

MARGO. Dad, I ca-

JEFF. Yes, you can. What did I promise you that one day after I picked you up from school? I will help you.

(**MARGO** *thinks for a moment.*)

MARGO. D-d-d-d-d-d-d-o you think he still plays stuff off of *Nebraska?*

JEFF. *(incredulous) Nebraska?*

(**JEFF** *puts his arm around her.*)

JEFF. So, you're gonna do yours on turtles?

MARGO. It's *t-t-t-tortoises,* Dad. Nnnot turtles.

JEFF. Same dif. But you're gonna do it? I shouldn't give these tickets back to Tanya?

MARGO. God, you've got me t-t-t-totally compromised. Yyyyou're just like B-b-bruce Springsteen's dad.

JEFF. How's that?

MARGO. When he was a t-t-t-teenager his dad kept telling him to c-c-cut his hair, b-b-b-but he wouldn't do it. B-b-b-b-but then one day he got in a motorcycle accident and his dad had a b-b-b-barber come to the hhhhospital and cut off all his hair while he was unconscious.

JEFF. That's a kind of an extreme comparison, don't you think?

MARGO. Nnnnno. You're, like, a t-t-total hair kamikaze or something.

JEFF. "Baby, we were booooorn to ruuuuuuun."

(**MARGO** *can smell his breath.*)

MARGO. Daaaad...quit being weird.

(**MARGO** *wriggles free.*)

MARGO. I've gotta go get ready for bed.

JEFF. Come on. We're having fun. Hey, since Mom's out of town, you can stay up and we could watch Conan if you wanted.

MARGO. Thhhhhat's okay. I'm p-p-p-p-pretty tired.

(She crumples up the exception slip and tosses it in the desk-side trash can.)

JEFF. Night, babe.

*(**MARGO** exits. **JEFF** checks his watch.)*

JEFF. Tell me this: What kind of teenager *chooses* to go to bed at nine?

When I picked her up from the school the next day, it was a "slam dunk." We got home and she went straight to her room to get ready for the presentation.

*(**MARGO** reenters with her book bag.)*

MARGO. D-d-d-dad?

JEFF. Yeah? How's it going in there?

MARGO. C-c-c-can you d-d-d-drive me to the library?

JEFF. What for?

MARGO. I need to g-get some b-b-books on iguanas.

JEFF. Iguanas? I thought we were doing tortoises.

MARGO. Yyyyyyeah. I changed my mind.

(beat)

JEFF. Why?

MARGO. I jjjjjjjust read the notes out loud in my rrrrroom and IIII d-decided they're not that interesting.

JEFF. Not interesting?

MARGO. Yeah, c-c-can we go now?

*(**JEFF** goes into her book bag and finds her notes on tortoises.)*

JEFF. Hold up. Let's hear your notes on tortoises, first.

MARGO. Right now?

JEFF. You spent all last night taking notes on them from your book; so I'm sure they can't be that boring.

MARGO. IIIIIIIIII…

JEFF. Hey. It's me. I promise you I won't be bored.

*(With a sigh, **MARGO** positions herself in front of the desk.)*

MARGO. One unique thing about t-t-t-t-t-tortoisest-hatseparatesthem/fffffrom other reptiles is the c-c-c-c-c-

JEFF. It's alright. Take your time.

MARGO. Fffuck!

JEFF. Come on. Chill out, Margo. It's-

MARGO. Wwwwwhen I think about them looking at me / all the words... Iiiiii...

JEFF. It's okay. You're just racing.

MARGO. I just want to get them all out as ssssoon as- And that's when I slip.

(**MARGO** *sits down at the chair on the opposite side of the desk and wraps her arms around her head.*)

JEFF. You do *not - need -* to hurry. Okay? For anyone.

Hey, listen. Margo, listen. You remember when we went to the Elko Speedway? You and me and Aunt Crystal and your cousins? You remember the race words I taught you?

MARGO. What are you talking about?

JEFF. "The caution period." You remember what that is?

MARGO. Wwwwhen you bring up Uncle Ted around Aunt Crystal?

JEFF. Very funny. No.

MARGO. I don't know. Wwwwhen there's a crash? What?

JEFF. Yeah. When there's a crash. When we were there, there was that crash.

Remember? And the pace car came out. And, when the pace car comes out, everybody that's trying to get to the front just has to slooooow down. All the cars have to get in a nice tidy row...and just take it easy.

(**MARGO** *looks up.*)

JEFF. Now the presentation probably looks like a ten-car pile-up right now, and all the words are trying to hurry to the front. We just need to slow things down and get them in a line.

MARGO. B-b-b-b-but, Dad, I can't focus on anything. I jusssssst start thinking about them thinking about me and I get all-

JEFF. And switching from tortoises to iguanas isn't going to fix that.

MARGO. Yes, it will. B-b-b-because it doesn't start on a p-p-plosive. T-t-t-Ts are my worst.

JEFF. You have to force yourself to get comfortable with plosives. You know James Earl Jones had a stutter so bad he refused to speak until he read his poem–

MARGO. His poem "Ode to Grapefruit" in front of the class. Yyyyyyyyou tell me this, like, every night.

JEFF. Because-

MARGO. And B-B-Bruce Willis and Bo Jackson and blah blah—

JEFF. *Because* he got comfortable by reciting something he cared about. You can't just spend your life trying to avoid talking about things that are important to you.

MARGO. B-b-b-b-but if I slip up, I'll embarrass myself.

JEFF. Okay: *yes.* If you slip up you *will* embarrass yourself. But that's okay.

MARGO. Why?

JEFF. Because we're going to make it so you don't slip up.

(**JEFF** *opens up his drawer and pulls out some index cards.*)

Here's what we'll do…take your notes for the presentation, okay? And just break them down into smaller pieces and write them out on these index cards.

MARGO. D-d-dad, this is stupid. It's nnnnot going to work.

JEFF. It'll be just like the teleprompter at the studio I showed you. That thing saves my butt because it gives me something small to focus on.

MARGO. B-b-b-b-but all it is is sssssssmaller pieces of p-p-paper.

JEFF. Just humor me. If it doesn't work, fine. You don't have to do the presentation. We can still go see the Boss and I'll be a big idiot. Whatever. I just want to show you that you can do this, okay?

(**MARGO** *takes the note cards and transcribes her notes while* **JEFF** *speaks.*)

(*to audience*) Plosives, in case you're wondering are consonants with the little explosions of air: Ts, Ks, Ps, etc. Even in the house, if Margo had to start a sentence on a plosive, she was toast. But, she'd taught herself to talk around them so that she'd never have to start on them.

MARGO. Alright. I'm done.

JEFF. Okay. Let's hear it.

(**MARGO** *stands up again to present. She's holding the index cards this time. She takes a deep breath.*)

MARGO. A unique thing about t-t-t...

JEFF. You can do—

(**MARGO** *puts up her hand to silence him.*)

MARGO. (*quietly*) One. Two. Three... A unique thing about tortoises that separates them from other reptiles is the c-carapace. The carapace is a convex arrangement of hard bony plates that c-c-c-c...that *shield* the tortoise from injury. When it hides in the carapace, the tortoise is safe from sssurprisingly severe injuries.

(**MARGO** *looks up, excitedly.*)

It's working.

JEFF. Yesssss! You, my beautiful daughter, are ready for tomorrow!

MARGO. I think I am.

JEFF. What was that thing you did? Were you counting?

MARGO. Yyyyyeah.

JEFF. Is that something your speech therapist told you about?

MARGO. Nnnno. I made it up for when there are too many things to think about to t-t-t... *Speak* well. It helps me ffffocus so I don't *(intentionally stuttering)* "stuh, stuh, stuh, stutter" so much.

JEFF. Funny. That works?

MARGO. Nnno matter how sssstressed out I get, I can always count okay. It c-c-calms me down so that b-b-by the time I get up to seven, I can figure out what to say.

JEFF. You know, TV producers always count *down*.

MARGO. B-b-b-but you don't have anywhere to go after one. Thhhhhere's too much pressure.

JEFF. I guess if you're counting down, you'd better know exactly what you're saying.

MARGO. Yeah...

JEFF. That's great, babe. Listen, I think there are a few things I feel like we could tweak up a little bit in your cards, though.

MARGO. Really? I think they're al–

JEFF. Come ooonnnn.

MARGO. IIIIIIIII think they're okay. B-b-besides, I n-need to go to sl–

JEFF. Come-on-come-on-come-on-come-on-come-on. Let me make a- write down a few suggestions.

MARGO. It's nine. I'm t-too tired to worry about–

JEFF. Who said *you* had to worry about anything? You just go to bed and I'll leave these for you in the morning. *(to audience)* God. Did you see that? I interrupted every fucking thing she said.

*(**MARGO** exits.)*

Anyway, I slaved over those cards and edited a few things here and there. Made sure all the terms were explained correctly. And - god, how late in the night must it have been for this to seem like a good idea - I scribbled little affirmations on the cards. Smiley faces, hearts, a few Springsteen lyrics. I found some stick-ers and put them on there. And, I put them all in an envelope and I wrote on the envelope, "Just remember how much your mother and I love you and let that be a pace car for you!" And I slipped it underneath her plate at the breakfast table, where she'd be sure to see them the next day.

JEFF. That's right… "Let that be a pace car for you." Now, I know what you're thinking. You're thinking, "No way Jeff came up with anything that eloquent and cogent." Well, my friends, I don't mind telling you that I was *exactly* that eloquent and cogent.

You might say that was one of the upsides of my problem. No shortage of words and metaphors. I was a veritable treasure trove of wisdom nuggets. Of course, it had its drawbacks.

(While he speaks, JEFF grabs one of the aquariums from the pet store and brings it over to the kitchen table.)

So, I proceeded to get royally fucked up that night. I woke up the next morning still a little drunk; so I called in sick to the studio. It wasn't uncommon around that time for the news anchor to utter the words "Jeff's got the night off." And, I decided that I'd spend the day putting together a little surprise for her. I bought a nice tank and a baby tortoise. So, I set it up on the kitchen table and threw a sheet over it to make it a surprise. You know, on top of the Boss tickets. Overkill, maybe. But I'd more or less forgotten her birthday that year, so why not go all out.

(JEFF sits down on his desk and picks up his mug, which he raises)

And, naturally….

(He takes a sip.)

(MARGO enters with her book bag. JEFF looks up.)

Hey, there she is… Wait, Margo, what are you doing here? I'm supposed to pick you up in an hour. You left early?

MARGO. Wwwwwwwwwhat do you think?

(**MARGO** *just stares at him. She's holding an envelope in her hand.*)

JEFF. Well? Are you gonna keep me, like, waiting in suspense? What kind of shot was today?

MARGO. D-d-d-d-d-d-does it look lllllllike it was slam d-d-dunk, Dad?

JEFF. Did the presentation not go well?

(**MARGO** *scoffs and walks up to* **JEFF** *and holds out the envelope.* **JEFF** *opens it enough to see that it's the index cards.*)

Did Mr. Kapsner not let you use the note cards?

(**MARGO** *starts to exit and* **JEFF** *looks at the cards and calls after her.*)

Wait, honey. Don't go. We can talk about it.
Did you slip? Is that it?

(**MARGO** *stops and turns around.*)

Don't be upset. I got you a pressie.

(*She stares back at him as he crosses to the table.*)

I was going to hide it here 'til after dinner. But...

(**JEFF** *pulls the sheet off of the aquarium, revealing it to* **MARGO**.)

I took the day off so I could give it to you tonight.

(**MARGO** *looks at it, still angry. Sure enough, there's a tortoise crawling around inside.*)

You know why I got all this for you? Because I love you and I just want you to be happy.

(**MARGO** *tries to say something to* **JEFF**, *but can't get it out.*)

MARGO. (*almost inaudibly*) IIIIIIIIIIIIIIIIIIIIIIIIII...

JEFF. And it's no big deal if you slipped. I do it on the air all the time. Look, I'll show you...
It's not a buh buh buh big deal.

(silence)

JEFF. I... I'm sorry. It's a joke, alright? I just want it to be so you know it's not so- so serious...

Margo, say something?

MARGO. (...)

JEFF. Babe? Are you okay?

(**MARGO** *looks at* **JEFF**, *hurt, and then punches the aquarium. The glass on the front panel spider-webs.* **MARGO** *storms out.*)

Margo!

(**JEFF** *picks up one of the index cards and crushes it in his hand.*)

(to audience) It was the index cards I'd made corrections to. Obviously.

In red, felt-tip pen, she'd underlined every single place where I'd made a new sentence that started with a plosive. There were fifteen. This was the day the little assholes at school gave her the name "Machine Gun Margo."

(**JEFF** *moves the driver's seat back to its position within the cabin.*)

She didn't speak for months. To anyone. And after two months of silence, Melissa and I decided maybe it'd be a good idea for Margo to go and live with her Aunt Crystal for a little while. She didn't utter another word in our house until after Melissa and I separated and I didn't live there anymore. Because of me. And that's why it's my responsibility - mine and not anyone else's - to do what I'm doing.

And what *am* I doing? I want to take this broken box and put it back together with her. We don't have to say *anything* if she doesn't want. It's symbolic, you know? Symbolic of the fact that even this can be a house again. And then, I want her to see this little reptile stumbling around and getting bumped and not getting it right.

JEFF. *(cont.)* But it's *okay*. Because she's beautiful and we love her. And we love her even more when she's not hiding in that shell. It's hokey. I know it's hokey. But it's what I'm *feeling*. And that's exactly it. I never let the hokey stuff - the soft goopy stuff - out. And I started to do it today and I don't know when I've ever felt more *alive*. Ted showed me; and now I want to show her. It's like the Boss says in "Born to Run": "The highway's jammed with broken heroes on a last chance power drive." And mine is to show her what I didn't get to show her last time.

You know, Fran Tarkenton, best quarterback Minnesota ever had, went to the Super Bowl with the Vikings not once, not twice, but *three* times. And - that talented fucking asshole - you know how many rings he has? Zero. He couldn't come through *any* of those three times. Now, I've fouled up... I've fouled up big. But Ted's right: I never blow a chance more than once.

(JEFF parks the car, gets out and looks in the direction of the house. JEFF crosses to the Twin Cities Map and points to a location in Golden Valley.)

So, that's why I rolled up to Melissa's house, here. I'd stored the old terrarium somewhere in the garage. Although Mel's lights were on, her car definitely wasn't there, so the coast was clear.

Now, I'm sure you're probably thinking, "Jeff. Breaking into your ex-wife's house? I don't know about that." Well, for one, I need that terrarium and that address. For another, we're on good terms even though we're separated, and I feel like she wouldn't be terribly pissed if she ever found out. And, for a third, I know she's got a key hidden under the mat.

(JEFF grabs the turtle bag out of the back seat and walks up to the stage left door. He knocks and peers though the window to see if anyone's home. After a moment there's no response, so he kicks back the doormat to find a key.)

JEFF. Easy-peasy, lemon squeezy.

*(As **JEFF** is leaning over to grab the hidden key, the door opens and **PETER** is standing there in his robe. He has some cash in his hand.)*

PETER. Hey, how's…

JEFF. Ah! Jesus!

PETER. Oh… Jeff. Hey.

*(**PETER** pulls the maneuver where you step outside and close the door behind you.)*

PETER. What, uh, what're you doing here, Jeff?

JEFF. I'd ask you the same thing, Peter.

PETER. I'm house-sitting. My sister's out of town.

JEFF. You expecting someone?

PETER. No…Just ordered a pizza. Assumed this was it.

JEFF. Whoa. You got a hot date inside or something?

PETER. What? What are you talking—

JEFF. You're doing the old step-outside-close-behind.

PETER. What? No. No… *(beat)*

*(**JEFF** holds up the bag with the turtle in it.)*

JEFF. Great. Do you mind if I come in, then? I just picked this up from the hot bar at Whole Foods, I don't want it to freeze.

PETER. Sorry, what do you want?

JEFF. There's something in the garage I need to get. Sorry to bug you; I just need it.

PETER. God, Jeff, it's going on ten. You need it at / this late hour?

JEFF. It's not even a quarter after nine.

PETER. It's a work night.

JEFF. Yeah, I see you're in your fancy robe and all. It won't take a minute. Just…
(sniffs) What's that smell?

PETER. Maybe you could come back tomorrow. I'm seriously *just* about to get into bed.

JEFF. I thought you said you just ordered a pizza.

> *(beat)*

All I need to do is find something in the garage really quickly. It'll be a three-minute operation.

PETER. Tell me where it is. Maybe I can just grab it for you.

JEFF. I'm not positive where. I need to look for it.

PETER. You're not positive? *(sighs)* Give me a call tomorrow and you can come over when I get off of work or something. You don't just show up at people's houses like this, expecting–

JEFF. Are you stoned?

> *(beat)*

PETER. Jeff, that's silly.

JEFF. I see. Big sister's out of town. So–

PETER. Oh, come off it.

JEFF. Alright, let me in before I call Mel and tell her what goes on in her house when she's away.

> *(beat)*

PETER. Come on.

> *(**PETER** opens the door behind him and walks in. **JEFF** follows, closing the door.)*

JEFF. Smells like freshman year in here.

> *(**PETER** turns shoots **JEFF** a look.)*

Sorry. I'm sure you're probably impatient to chill out and watch *Dark Crystal* on *my* flat screen.

PETER. Actually, I was just waiting for the ten o'clock news to come on Channel 9.

JEFF. Oh. I'm taking the ten o'clock off tonight.

PETER. We all need a night off sometimes. What is it you're looking for?

JEFF. My old aquarium. I'm gonna go poke my head in there.

PETER. The broken one?

JEFF. I'm gonna repair it.

PETER. Wow…wait. Did you know Mel was out of town?

JEFF. No. I thought she'd be here.

(**JEFF** *crosses to the garage.* **PETER** *follows.* **JEFF** *walks into the garage and starts to search the shelves while* **PETER** *stands sentry in the doorway.*)

PETER. Hot bar, huh? Were you planning on eating here?

JEFF. No. It's below zero out there. I just didn't want it to freeze in the car.

PETER. Freeze? How long are you planning on being here?

JEFF. Don't worry, Peter. I have no desire to prolong the experience of feeling like a trespasser in my own house.

PETER. No…I didn't mean it like that. Actually, I'm glad you're here.

(**JEFF** *grabs a step-ladder to access the high shelves in the garage. While he sets it up, he notices that* **PETER**'*s not going anywhere.*)

JEFF. You can leave me to look for it.

PETER. No, I'll stick around. We haven't talked in a while. It's not often we get this experience. Just you and me.

JEFF. Something you've been crossing your fingers for?

PETER. Well, you're the biggest celebrity I know. And, we haven't really had a lot of one-on-one since you two separated. And, the whole family situation now's so unique, you know? It's interesting…

JEFF. How's that?

PETER. Well, you and Mel are separated; but you two still seem to get along so well. I mean, all of your time in and out of recovery, she's just been, you know, really impressively attentive. Commendable, isn't it?

JEFF. Yeah. That's Mel for you. Hey, speaking of which, you mind if I check for an address in her book?

PETER. Can't help you out with that. I don't know where her address book is.

JEFF. That's okay. I think–

PETER. Wait. What address are you looking for?

JEFF. Ted's.

PETER. Ted's? I hear he's off the wagon.

JEFF. I wouldn't know, Peter.

PETER. You lucked out. Crystal sure doesn't care for Ted the way Mel does for you. It's weird…having two sisters who've gone through this.

JEFF. Must be difficult for you.

PETER. So, what've you been up to today, Jeff?

JEFF. Nothing…just thinking about getting this aquarium set up in my den. Why?

PETER. I've just been thinking about you tonight.

JEFF. Why's that?

PETER. Today's kind of a big day, isn't it?

JEFF. How do you mean?

PETER. Jesus, man…

The Santana trade!

JEFF. Oh! Right.

PETER. Come on! The Winter Conferences started / today.

JEFF. The Winter Meetings. Yeah.

PETER. Star Tribune's cover story is whether the Twins trade him.

JEFF. Yeah… It's a… pretty big deal. You know, you ask me, he's gone already.

He'll be in pinstripes by Opening Day.

PETER. Yeah? You bent out of shape about that?

JEFF. We're a small market team; this is the way Minnesota sports goes. Boys turn into men in the Metrodome and the Target Center and then they go away forever. Chuck Knoblauch, Randy Moss, A.J. Pierzinski, Kevin Garnett. That douchebag Torii Hunter just signed with the Angels.

PETER. Fran Tarkenton, too, right?

(JEFF *smiles at this as he pushes a box aside and sees the aquarium with the broken pane.*)

JEFF. Oh, yeah. It's just like the Boss says in "Thunder Road": "It's a town full of losers and I'm pulling out of here to win."

Hey! Look! There it is.

PETER. Good. Good. Here, hand it over.

(JEFF *hands it down to* PETER *and then climbs down the step-ladder.* PETER *hands the tank back to him.*)

JEFF. Thanks, Peter.

PETER. Sure. Come on. It's cold out here.

JEFF. Yeah. Brr…

(PETER *opens the door to the house, lets* JEFF *through and closes it behind them.*)

PETER. Yeah. So, they become men and they go away. So interesting…

JEFF. Yeah. I didn't know you followed that stuff.

PETER. You know, I don't. But I tuned into the six o'clock news tonight to see if you'd be covering that.

JEFF. Oh. Yeah. Like I said, I took the night off.

PETER. You said you took the ten o'clock off…

JEFF. Well, I took them both.

PETER. Clearly. Where they usually introduce your "Sports Wrap," they said you were out for the week.

JEFF. No, that's not right. I'm not out for… Tonight, yeah. Maybe tomorrow.

PETER. Good, because I heard that and, naturally, I was wondering if you were alright.

JEFF. Yeah, no, I'm fine. You tell Mel about that?

PETER. No. I was just curious why you'd be out for the week. I know you haven't been traveling since you went to Hazelden.

JEFF. Good, I don't want her to worry. You know how she is.

PETER. Oh, of course. That is what she does…worries about you. Which is crazy, really. Because she's always talking about how you've been sober for over two years.

JEFF. Your sister's a very supportive person. Very supportive.

PETER. You know what I realized must be frustrating for you? That even when you've been sober for that long, nobody else can ever really know for sure.

JEFF. Yeah.

PETER. So, why'd they say all week?

JEFF. How should I know, Peter?

PETER. I've got to ask because, well… You've gotta admit, this situation… You're acting awfully funny.

JEFF. You're the one sneaking spliffs in your sister's house while she's out of town.

PETER. Well, Jeff, Mel's not crazy about drugs and booze these days. I can hardly have a glass of Pinot Grigio at dinner without her shoulders tensing up.

No offense, Jeff, but maybe you can guess why that is.

JEFF. Alright, Peter. I'm gonna get out of your hair, alright? Let me just get that address and I'll be on my way.

PETER. No.

JEFF. What?

PETER. What's up with the time off?

JEFF. Not that it's any of your business, but I'm taking a few vacation days to work on some things. You ever take those over at Pep Boys?

PETER. It is not a Pep Boys, Jeff. It's independently owned.

JEFF. Come on, Peter. I need Ted's address.

PETER. Okay. Call Mel and ask permission.

JEFF. No. That's ridiculous. I'm not going to bother Mel with this.

PETER. Weren't you going to bother her by showing up at her door at ten o'clock?

JEFF. Nine fifteen.

PETER. It really goes to show you how much she'll do for–

JEFF. What is the problem here, Peter?

PETER. You think I forgot what day it is? Jeff?
Because unless you want to go back and tell me you knew Mel was out of town, then you're telling me Mel's okay with you dropping in unannounced to pull a last minute birthday gift for Margo off the scrap heap. And I will not let that happen.

JEFF. It's *my* aquarium.

PETER. That's not what I'm talking about. I don't give a shit about that. I want you to take that.

JEFF. Yeah?

PETER. Oh, yeah.

JEFF. Why's that?

PETER. For one, because it's a piece of trash and I'm not so sure what you're gonna do with that aquarium since you don't have Margo's address. (Nice try with the Ted thing.) And, second, because now I can explain to Mel that I was watching the news and saw that you missed your first broadcast in years for some mystery reason. That'll probably ring plenty of bells. And that you came over here drunk at ten o'clock on a weeknight and stole that aquarium - that aquarium that... You know, who in their right mind would want a busted aquarium?

JEFF. Why would you tell her that?

PETER. Because my sister can't move on like this. She doesn't date for fear of upsetting your recovery, if that's even the word for it. I ask her to go on vacation with me, she tells me, "I don't know if that's a good idea yet. If something happened with Jeff, who'd be there for him?"

JEFF. So, her trademark compassion's not hereditary, is it?

PETER. Because this isn't fair. And because I know she won't stop talking to you on her own.

JEFF. You can't stop me from talking to her. Or vice versa. You're not-

PETER. Get this straight, Jeff: You-are-not-her-husband-anymore.

JEFF. I never… You're way out of line. This is completely inappropriate. Now, I want that ad–

PETER. Inappropriate? What about drunk driving in her Oldsmobile?

JEFF. I'm– I'm not drunk, Peter! Stop saying that!

PETER. No? You're not? That's so weird. I could've sworn you came over here drunk. Yeah, about 10 o'clock. And I tried to tell you it was too late; but you stuck your foot in the door so I couldn't close it - shoved your way through the front door to grab that aquarium. Then, God, you nearly took out the mailbox backing out of the driveway.

JEFF. I have been sober for two and a half years.

PETER. Well, no one can ever really know for sure, can they?

JEFF. You're a real piece of work, Peter.

PETER. I care about you, Jeff. I *love* you. But that gets exhausted in a way that my love for Mel doesn't. And I'm not going to keep watching you elbow your way into her life. And if I have to use a sleazy tactic, so be–

(*A* **PIZZA GUY** *arrives at the door and the doorbell rings.* **PETER** *freezes, unsure of whether to leave* **JEFF** *alone in the room with the address book.*)

(*beat*)

PETER. Why don't you come with me to the door?

(**JEFF** *leans back against the wall.*)

JEFF. Mm… You know, I would, but I sure did hurt my foot sticking it in the door like that.

(*The doorbell rings again.*)

Below zero, Peter. Pizza's probably getting cold.

PETER. Shit.

(PETER hurriedly exits to pay for his pizza. As PETER is dealing with the PIZZA GUY, JEFF quickly goes into the bookshelf and grabs the address book. Neither part of the house is in view of the other.)

PETER. Hey. How much?

JEFF. Come on, come on... Where is she?   PIZZA GUY. Uhh... Twelve and thirteen cents.

(PETER cranes his neck, but can't see what JEFF is up to in the next room.)

PETER. You got change? Hurry it up.

(JEFF finds the right page in the address book and scribbles down the address on a piece of scrap paper.)

PIZZA GUY. Yeah... Hold up. For twenty?   JEFF. 415 Fifth Avenue... 415 Fifth Avenue... 415 Fifth Avenue...

PETER. Forget it. Forget it. Here.

(PETER grabs the pizza and closes the door just as JEFF is wedging the address book back onto the shelf.)

(PETER enters right as JEFF has re-assumed his original position, leaning against the wall. He's smiling now, though.)

PETER. What did you do?

JEFF. Nothing. You know what? I think I've got everything I need. So, if you'll excuse me.

(JEFF places the turtle bag into the terrarium and makes to leave.)

PETER. Jeff, I don't care what kind of nutcase amends-making mission you're on; I don't want you going over there. That's Margo's home and she doesn't want you to have anything to do with it, you got that?

JEFF. Excuse me.

PETER. She doesn't need to get any more screwed up than she already is. There's nothing you can say to fix things.

(JEFF *gives* **PETER** *a condescending pat on the chest.*)

JEFF. I'll watch out for the mailbox, Peter. Enjoy the Meat-Lovers, alright?

(JEFF *walks out the front door and heads towards the car.* **PETER** *calls out the door after him.*)

PETER. Mel's going to hear about this.

(JEFF *sets the aquarium in the back of the car and gets back in the driver's seat.* **PETER** *closes the door and exits. The lights go down on the house.*)

JEFF. *(to audience)* He's wrong. There are things that I can say to her. There's always something you can say. And when he said that, that's when I decided the third of the three "right theres" had to happen.

(JEFF *now pulls out a flask-sized bottle of Maker's Mark. He pours about half its contents into his travel mug. He takes the shot.*)

(to audience) That probably seems like a bad idea... But, I can't let Peter be right. I have to be able to say it all without holding back. If I had been able to *say* some of the things I was *thinking* that day in the car... Maybe I could have changed something.

(JEFF *gets up and looks out at the site, which is off the driver's side of the vehicle.*)

And now, from the curb outside of Margo's house, I can see the terrifyingly bright construction lights flickering between the trees. I haven't ventured across the river much since the bridge collapsed in August, so I almost never see the site of the accident.

35-W just vanished, dropping about a hundred cars onto the banks and into the river. It's scary to think about: your car slowly filling up with pebbles and sand, water climbing the glass.

A reporter friend of mine told me that the bridge itself could've been fine on its gusset plates. But, there were black ice problems with the bridge, so they patched it up with an extra two-inch layer of concrete.

(*JEFF sits back down in the driver's seat and takes the wheel. He maneuvers the car to a curb and looks out through the passenger's side window.*)

JEFF. And, as I consider whether it was the patching up that might have caused the catastrophe, I pop one last Altoid. And that about brings us up to speed...

(*JEFF pops an Altoid in his mouth and counts to seven.*)

One. Two. Three. Four. Five. Six. Seven.

(*He gets out of the car and nervously places the turtle, the bag of gear and the pane of glass into the busted aquarium and carries it to the door.*)

(*He then approaches the stage left door and pauses a moment before finally knocking.*)

JEFF. Here we go...

(*After a moment, **BRIAN**, a guy in his early twenties, answers the door in a University of St. Thomas sweatshirt.*)

BRIAN. Hi.

JEFF. Hi.

BRIAN. Can I help you with something?

JEFF. Sorry, yeah. I spaced. Is...is this Margo's place? Does she live here?

BRIAN. Yeah. This is her place. She's not here right now; I'm just waiting for her.

JEFF. Um...when'll she be in?

BRIAN. I don't know. Probably not that long.

JEFF. Tell you what. It's freezing out here. Would you mind if I waited for her inside?

BRIAN. Who are you?

JEFF. I'm her father.

BRIAN. Oh...yeah. I don't know about that.

JEFF. Don't know about what?

BRIAN. Listen, I should really get this cake from the oven. So...

(BRIAN *starts to close the door, but* JEFF *puts his foot in it.*)

BRIAN. Your foot's-

JEFF. Please. She knows I'm coming.

BRIAN. I was under the impression you didn't know where she was living.

JEFF. No, no. Where do you think I got her address? Her mother certainly didn't give it to me. I talked to her.

BRIAN. You talked to her?

JEFF. Well. E-mailed. I'm sorry. Are you-I'm guessing you're the boyfriend? Am I right on that?

BRIAN. Yeah.

JEFF. And she didn't tell you about this?

BRIAN. No, she didn't.

JEFF. Shoot. Well, I can totally sympathize with your position here. I'm sure you've heard plenty of stories about what a drunk a-hole Margo's old man is; and if I were in your shoes, I'm not sure what I'd do, either. So, just to clear the air, I've been on the wagon for over two years now. I'm not sure if Margo told you that either.

BRIAN. Yeah, I mean, it doesn't seem like you're drinking. But it was my *understanding* that that didn't matter. As far as Margo was concerned.

JEFF. Yeah, she and I already worked that out. She laid some ground rules and told me this wasn't going to be a big thing. She said I could come over and give her her birthday present and that'd be it.

Look at me; I'm not here to cause any trouble.

BRIAN. Right. Well, come in out of the cold, then.

(BRIAN *opens the door enough to permit* JEFF. JEFF *picks up the aquarium and walks in.*)

JEFF. Thanks.

(As JEFF *walks in, he sees that* BRIAN's *cake is already set out on the dining room table.*)

JEFF. It's good to meet you. I'm Jeff.

BRIAN. Brian.

JEFF. Brian, the Tommie. Cool. So, how long have you and Margo been together?

BRIAN. How'd you know I was at St. Thomas?

(*JEFF points at* **BRIAN***'s shirt.*)

BRIAN. Oh, right. I've been seeing Margo for about six months.

JEFF. Whoa. That's a good-looking cake, Brian. You bake that yourself?

BRIAN. Yeah…I guess Margo should be coming home from school pretty quick.

JEFF. What's the class?

BRIAN. It's a communications course. You know, you can set that down anywhere you like.

JEFF. Great. Somewhere out of the way maybe.

BRIAN. You could tuck it down there near that amp if you want.

(*JEFF does so.*)

JEFF. Is this Margo's? Did she pick up guitar?

BRIAN. No, that's mine.

JEFF. Oh. So you live here.

BRIAN. Yeah. I was moving out of my old place near campus at the end of last school year and the timing just worked out.

JEFF. So. Also six months ago. *(only kind of under his breath)* Can't beat free rent, can you?

BRIAN. What?

JEFF. Nothing. Where'd you guys meet?

BRIAN. Where'd we meet? Just around. Through friends.

(*Beat.* **JEFF** *smiles.*)

JEFF. Right. So, Brian, you'd probably be the best person for me to ask. I'd like to ask before Margo gets here. What's the matter?

BRIAN. I'm sorry?

JEFF. Part of the reason I'm over here is I that heard she's been acting, I don't know, strangely.

BRIAN. Where'd you hear that?

JEFF. One of her uncles.

BRIAN. What do you mean "strangely"?

JEFF. Quiet.

BRIAN. Quiet? I guess I don't know what you're saying exactly. Someone told you she hasn't been talkative lately?

JEFF. No, it's a bigger deal than that.

You may have noticed she has a stutter.

BRIAN. Well. Yeah.

JEFF. There was this time that she got teased for it at school and she just – zzzzzzzip – pulled the curtain. Stopped talking to anybody. Even me and her mom. So, naturally, when I heard that she's been quiet – like, wasn't even talking to her own family at the wedding last week – I became concerned.

BRIAN. You know, I know Margo pretty well. And, I mean, you're concerned about something you heard. I understand. I just don't think she's acting all that weird.

JEFF. No? And you'd notice, too, being her boyfriend. Having her best interest at heart.

BRIAN. What's up with that fish tank?

JEFF. It's a terrarium. It's my birthday gift for Margo.

BRIAN. What happened to it? Did you slip outside or something?

JEFF. No. It was already broken. I'm gonna repair it. It's just kind of a, I don't know, symbolic thing.

BRIAN. Symbolic of what?

JEFF. It's hard to explain. It's…

Hey, do you have a rest room I could use?

BRIAN. Sure. It's right there.

(**BRIAN** *points to the stage right door.* **JEFF** *walks through, into the rest room, leaving* **BRIAN** *alone.*)

JEFF. Thanks.

> (JEFF *goes to the bathroom and closes the door behind him.*)

JEFF. Come on, Jeff. Just count... Come on...

> (JEFF *looks in the mirror and composes himself.*)

> (BRIAN *pulls out his phone and dials.*)

BRIAN. Hey, Margo, don't come right home, okay? Call me first. It's important.
Something-

> (*There's a jingling of keys and the front door opens.*)

> (MARGO *passes through it. As she enters, she's of a warmer disposition than we've seen from her. She's confident and speaks without impediment.*)

JEFF. One... Two...

MARGO. Babycakes! I'm home.

JEFF. ...Three... Four...

> (BRIAN *crosses to greet her.*)

BRIAN. Hey...

MARGO. Heyyyyy. How's my man?

> (JEFF *hears this and realizes that* MARGO *is home.*)

BRIAN. I was hoping to catch you-

MARGO. Cake! You *did* make it. *Briannnn.* This is so nice! Is this the red velvet?

BRIAN. It is. I was hoping to catch you before you walked in.

> (JEFF *puts his ear to the door and listens.*)

MARGO. To hide your handiwork? Nuh-uh...

BRIAN. Margo-

MARGO. I don't know if I told you this the last time you made that cake; but when I worked in that bakery, they'd cut the tops off the red velvet cakes to just leave the fluffiest parts, and they'd send us home with these bags *full* of the tops and bottoms of–

BRIAN. Right. And they'd send you home with the tops and bottoms. Margo, did you invite anyone over tonight?

(**MARGO** *crosses to the bowl of frosting next to the cake. She gets a taste on her finger.*)

MARGO. Ha. Mom took me out for lunch before she went out of town; so don't worry. Butter cream frosting!

BRIAN. Your mom? No. I'm asking because your...

(*Seeing* **JEFF** *emerge from the restroom,* **BRIAN** *stops talking.*)

MARGO. You look so serious. What?

(**MARGO** *turns around to see* **JEFF**.)

JEFF. Hi. Margo.
Happy birthday.

MARGO. What's he doing here?

BRIAN. I was trying to ask... You didn't know?

MARGO. Hhhe's not ssssupposed to know... God.

BRIAN. He said the two of you-

MARGO. What are you doing here, Dad?

JEFF. I just wanted to check in on you.

MARGO. Why?

JEFF. Just to do something nice. Maybe talk.

MARGO. We *don't* talk.

BRIAN. Alright. There's been a misunderstanding here. This is my fault. But it'd probably be best if you-

MARGO. Brian, mmaybe you could just give us a second. Okay?

BRIAN. Are you sure?

MARGO. Yeah. I'm fine.

BRIAN. Okay. I'm in the next room if you need me.

(**BRIAN** *exits.*)

JEFF. So... Night class on your birthday? That's a bum deal.

MARGO. So you got Brian to let you in.

JEFF. Yeah. I didn't realize your boyfriend was living here.

MARGO. Yeah.

JEFF. Did he really move in as soon as you guys started dating? That seems—

MARGO. Dad, it's not like that. He d-didn't even want to move in.

JEFF. Looks like he did anyway.

MARGO. B-b-because I convinced him to.

JEFF. Oh… I was nervous that-

MARGO. Nnnnot that it's any of your business. Thhhhis is my home. Why did you think it was okay to come to my home?

JEFF. I just heard…

MARGO. What?

JEFF. Sometimes I feel like you wouldn't be so quiet if it weren't for / me.

MARGO. Yyyyou're right.

(beat)

JEFF. Someone said you weren't talking too much these days. That it was just like the other time, when you were younger. So naturally I got worried and wanted to make sure ev-

MARGO. Who t-told you that?

JEFF. Uncle Ted.

MARGO. IIIIIIIIIIIIIII don't talk to Uncle Ted because he's always d-d-drunk, Dad.

JEFF. At the reception, though. He said you were completely silent. That you weren't talking to any-

MARGO. The reception? Iiiiis that what this is about? Everyone at that reception was drunk. I d-d-didn't feel like talking to them. I just wanted to get B-B-Brian out of there.

JEFF. But Uncle Ted made it sound like you were-

MARGO. Aaaaaaaaas you can see, I'm fine. So if thhhat's why you're here, thanks, but you can go. I'm not the ffffourteen years old girl you nnneeded to drive around after school. And I'd appreciate it if you didn't come around here anymore.

JEFF. Margo, please. I realized some things today. And I just wanted to come and give you this birthday present.

MARGO. You remembered?

JEFF. Yeah. I did.

MARGO. What birthday present?

JEFF. It's, what do you call it, interactive. Just look, real quick...

(**JEFF** *moves to where the aquarium is stuck and pulls it out. He places it on edge of the table next to the cake.*)

Do you remember it?

(**MARGO** *looks at him.*)

MARGO. Wow, D-d-dad. This is great. This b-brings back a lot of awesome memories.

JEFF. Look, I know it's weird. But I brought some glue and a new pane of glass and I wrote down some instructions. I thought maybe, if you want, you and I could fix it together.

MARGO. Fix it?

JEFF. I thought, if we fixed it, you might like it for your house. I don't know if you guys already have one.

MARGO. No, we d-don't. You got rocks and everything.

JEFF. You always used to say that every house should have one of these.

MARGO. I asked you to not t-try to get in touch with me or give me presents. I mean, I'm happy you remembered. And this is a really nice gesture.

JEFF. I know. You did. You're right. So let's not call it a birthday present and just call it what it is. An apology.

(**MARGO** *can't help it. She smiles.*)

MARGO. I d-don't know what to do with it once we repair it. I don't have any fish or anything.

JEFF. Well. Look what else... Close your eyes. Put out your hand.

*(**MARGO** looks at **JEFF** skeptically.)*

MARGO. Are you kidding?

JEFF. Come on. I'm not Springsteen's dad. It's not like I'm gonna cut your hair off while your eyes are closed.

*(**MARGO** chuckles slightly. She closes her eyes and puts out her hand. **JEFF** opens the plastic carton and puts the turtle in her cupped hand.)*

JEFF. I know how you like them.

MARGO. Oh, my god. It's moving. What is it?

JEFF. Open 'em.

(She opens her eyes and sees the turtle.)

MARGO. Iiiiiiiit's *tortoises*, Dad... Not turtles.
(realizing) Oh, God. Dad...

JEFF. Wait. No... It's not like that. Not one of those things where I forget.

MARGO. Yyyyou're drunk...

*(**MARGO** starts to back away.)*

JEFF. No, it's– I just couldn't get the tortoise tonight. We'll go there tomorrow. Just you and me. What do you say?

MARGO. (...)

JEFF. Margo? Say something.

*(**MARGO** tries to call out to **BRIAN**.)*

MARGO. B-b-b-b-b-b-b-b-b...

JEFF. It's a symbolic thing. We can put it back together together. Heh: "Together together." And the turtle fumbles around, right? But it's still beautiful.

*(While **JEFF** speaks, **MARGO** places the turtle inside the busted aquarium. **JEFF** notices this.)*

*(Hearing the glottal noise, **BRIAN** reenters.)*

BRIAN. Margo? Is everything okay?

MARGO. IIIIIIIII

JEFF. The tortoise isn't the point. The point is that I understand. I really understand now. And the…

BRIAN. What's the matter with her?

BRIAN. Margo, do you want him to leave?

MARGO. (…)

JEFF. When we sat in the car I was so stupid. It wasn't because I didn't care. I just couldn't say what I was feeling. See, I know. I know what it's like to not be able to say what you want to say.

BRIAN. Why isn't she saying anything?

BRIAN. Baby? Just tell me what you want.

(JEFF *gets between them and puts his hands on* MARGO*'s shoulders.*)

JEFF. Margo, say something. I want you to be able to talk. I don't want you to be like me. Come on. Please. I need to hear you.

MARGO. G-g-g-g-g-g-g-g-g-g

BRIAN. Jeff, she's not okay with that.

BRIAN. Jeff. You need to go.

JEFF. Go? Hey, Brian. Is this your place? Do you pay rent here? Do you-

BRIAN. No. Margo's mom takes-

JEFF. No, I do. I pay the rent here. So, I'm not going anywhere.

MARGO. WWWWWWWWWWW…

BRIAN. No. That can't be true.

JEFF. Shit. Look: the rent doesn't mean anything. It's still your house.

BRIAN. Jeff, seriously. You **MARGO**.
need to go.   Thhhhhhhhhhhhhhhhhh

    (**JEFF** *picks up the tube of glue and forces it into* **MARGO** *'s hand.*)

JEFF. Here. We don't have to say anything. I'll give you the glue and we'll rebuild this. Okay?

BRIAN. Jeff, leave her alone.

JEFF. Okay?

BRIAN. Margo, come on. Let's go.

    (**BRIAN** *moves take* **MARGO** *by the arm.*)

JEFF. Don't *touch* her.

    (**JEFF** *moves to block* **BRIAN** *'s movement. In doing so, he upsets the table.*)

    (*Both the aquarium and the cake fall to the floor. The aquarium and shatters with the turtle still inside.*)

JEFF. No!

BRIAN. Margo, come on. You'll cut yourself.

    (**BRIAN** *pulls* **MARGO** *to the side.*)

Margo? Are you all right?
Baby, please say something. Just count. Like you used to.

MARGO. *(almost indiscernible)* Ooooooooooooo... T-t-t-t-t-t-t-t-t-t-t....

BRIAN. I'm gonna take you to our room and get him out of here. Come on.

    (**BRIAN** *walks* **MARGO** *back toward the bedroom. She exits.*)

    (**BRIAN** *turns toward* **JEFF**.)

BRIAN. Get out of here, Jeff.

    (**BRIAN** *moves toward* **JEFF** *as if to rush him.*)

BRIAN. GET OUT OF HERE!

(**JEFF** *puts his hands up.*)

JEFF. It's okay! It's okay. I'm going.

(**JEFF** *turns and leaves the house. He crosses to the car. He sits down and takes a moment to collect himself.*)

I just keep doing this to you, Margo.
I just keep doing this...

(**JEFF** *starts the car.*)

JEFF. But I know what I need to do.

(**MARGO** *enters. She is once again fourteen years old. She has her backpack. It's not exactly a memory and not exactly a daydream. Something in between. A bringing of the past into the present.*)

MARGO. Hey, P-p-p-pops.

JEFF. Hey, Margo.

(**MARGO** *plunks down into the passenger's seat.*)

MARGO. Aaaaaask me. Come on. Ask me!

JEFF. Alright. Okay. What kind of shot was today, babe?

MARGO. Sssssslam dunk!

JEFF. No kidding!

MARGO. Yyyyyyeah. C-c-c-can we go for a drive b-before you go to work?

JEFF. We do that when you've had an air ball, babe. I've gotta get to the studio.

MARGO. B-b-b-but I want to tell you what happened with C-C-Clarissa.

JEFF. You've got the whole ride to the house to fit it in. Now this is that tall girl in your grade?

MARGO. Yeah. Sssssso, we were d-d-doing the circuit thing in gym, where there are a b-b-bunch of different stations. Aaaaand I was having a hard time catching the b-b-ball at the football station. Aaaaand Clarissa who's, like, a total b-b-beyotch, was all—

JEFF. Margo.

MARGO. Sorry. She was all, "Hey, Mmmargo. Maybe you should've just stuck t-t-to one sport. I know it's hard for ssssssstutterers to focus on more than one thing at a t-t-time."

And I was, like, "T-t-tell that to B-B-Bo Jackson."

JEFF. You did that? Really?

MARGO. Yeah.

JEFF. That's… that's great.

MARGO. IIIIIIII just wish I wasn't such a screw-up. I shouldn't have ssssstarted on a T-T-T.

JEFF. Margo, don't say that. You are not the screw-up.

MARGO. D-d-d-dad, you can't go this way, the rrroad's closed.

JEFF. I'm serious. You're not a screw-up. You know that, right?

MARGO. The words p-p-probably sounded dumb, though.

JEFF. Well, Margo. Actions speak louder than words.

(**MARGO** *sees something through the windshield.*)

MARGO. Wwwwwait. Wwwwhy are there all those lights up there on the b-b-bridge?

JEFF. Alright. Time for you to hop out.

MARGO. D-d-dad, are you sure this is the rrrright way?

JEFF. Yes, Margo. Now come on. Your home's on this side of the river.

MARGO. Okay. Bye, Dad.

JEFF. Night, babe.

(**MARGO** *gets up from the passenger's seat and exits.*)

I finally found just the right thing to say.

(**JEFF** *closes his eyes.*)

Seven. Six. Five. Four. Three. Two. One.

(*lights out*)

END OF PLAY

JEFF'S ROUTE

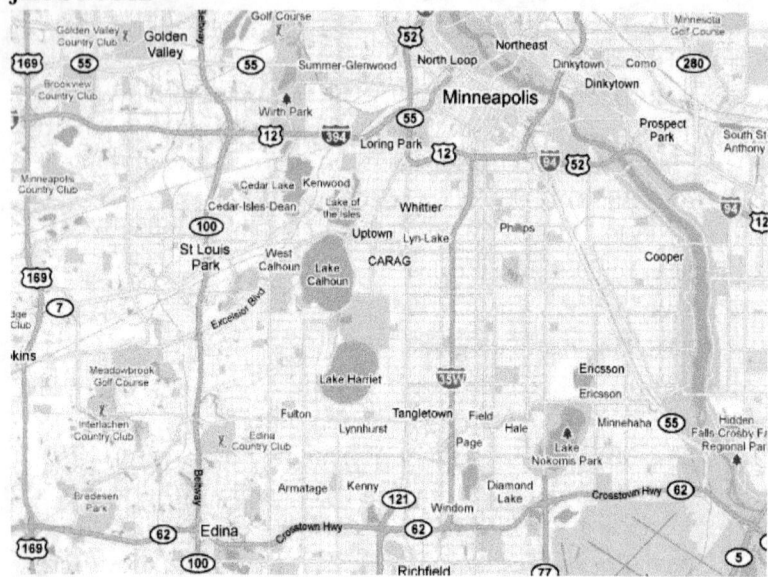

JEFF travels from Edina to St. Louis Park and Golden Valley via Highway 100. He then takes 100 back down to I-394, which he takes to I-35W to cross the Mississippi (see next map).

THE 35-W MISSISSIPPI RIVER BRIDGE AND SURROUNDING AREAS

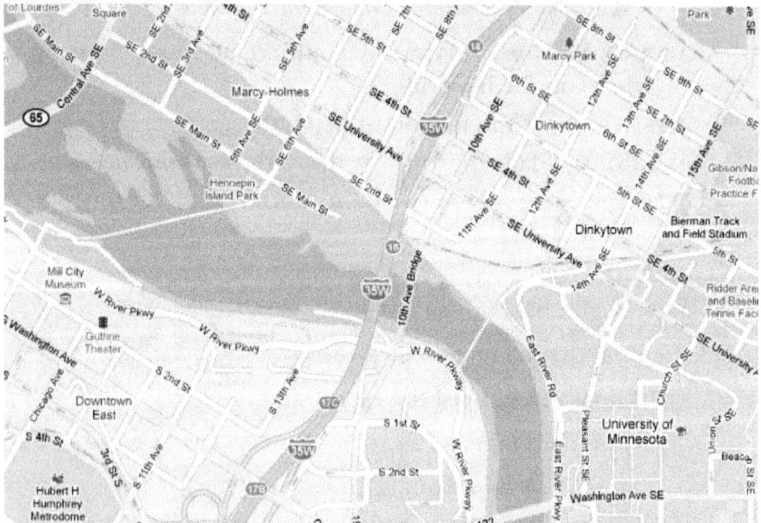

Here you can see the 10th Ave. Bridge, which runs alongside the I-35W Bridge. Just northwest of each is the Marcy-Holmes neighborhood, where Margo lives. Her place would be right around the intersection of SE 4th Street and SE 5th Avenue.

OTHER TITLES AVAILABLE FROM SAMUEL FRENCH

BATTLE HYMN

Jim Leonard

Dramatic Comedy / 4m, 1f with doubling / Unit Set

Winner! LA Weekly Award for Best New Play

Award-winning playwright Jim Leonard's latest, *Battle Hymn*, is the story of 16-year-old Martha's epic pregnancy and her incredible search for motherhood, meaning, and love in a war-torn American landscape. After being abandoned by her father, losing her true love and witnessing the horrors of the Civil War firsthand, Martha settles on one incontrovertible fact: She will not raise her baby in a blood-soaked, violent country. And so, Martha keeps traveling in search of a better world and a safe place to bring forth her child… this is easier said than done. From the mud and the blood of Fort Sumter to singing cows, San Francisco and the summer of love, Martha's journey embodies the tragedy, humor and hope that have helped shape the last 150 years of U.S. history.

"Refreshingly original, smart and engaging."
– LA Times

"Sinfully rich theatrical adventure infused with profoundly resonant social satire that produces visceral wonderment."
– Backstage West

"Leonard's writing is rich and often humorous, and he's skilled at creating memorable characters."
– Variety

OTHER TITLES AVAILABLE FROM SAMUEL FRENCH

A SMALL FIRE

Adam Bock

Drama / 2m, 2f / Interior

Adam Bock's meticulously crafted *A Small Fire* follows John and Emily Bridges, a long-married couple whose happy, middle-class lives are upended when Emily falls victim to a mysterious disease. As her senses are slowly stripped away – smell, taste, sight – Emily resolves to remain engaged with her community, relying on John to help her run her company and experience her daughter Jenny's wedding. But her stoic outlook reaches a breaking point when the disease steals her hearing, leaving her with nothing but touch to communicate with the world. Suddenly, she is completely dependant on the husband whose endless devotions she had always taken for granted.

"The play is…raucous, funny and unexpectedly touching, as we are made intimate witnesses to a frank demonstration of how much of life, of love and of happiness remain within reach even when so much appears to be lost."
– *The New York Times*

"*A Small Fire* is a small play, tightly focused and written close to the vest, but its small virtues are numerous and meaningful; in retrospect, they begin to loom very large."
– *Village Voice*

OTHER TITLES AVAILABLE FROM SAMUEL FRENCH

MAPLE AND VINE

Jordan Harrison

Dramatic Comedy / 2m, 2f / Multiple Sets

Katha and Ryu have become allergic to their 21st-century lives. After they meet a charismatic man from a community of 1950s re-enactors, they forsake cell phones and sushi for cigarettes and Tupperware parties. In this compulsively authentic world, Katha and Ryu are surprised by what their new neighbors - and they themselves - are willing to sacrifice for happiness.

"Piquantly funny, cleverly executed and darkly playful."
– *The New York Times*

"Jordan Harrison's *Maple and Vine* does everything a good play should do. It entertains. It makes you think....1950's conformity may not differ much from 2011's, but at least we have our conveniences. Harrison makes you weigh the costs and benefits of both eras without hitting you over the head with his own conclusion. You will enjoy reaching your own."
– *Theatre Louisville*

www.ingramcontent.com/pod-product-compliance
Lightning Source LLC
Chambersburg PA
CBHW070648120726
47909CB00004B/1626